# ELYMPICS

Poems by **X. J. KENNEDY**

Pictures by **GRAHAM PERCY**

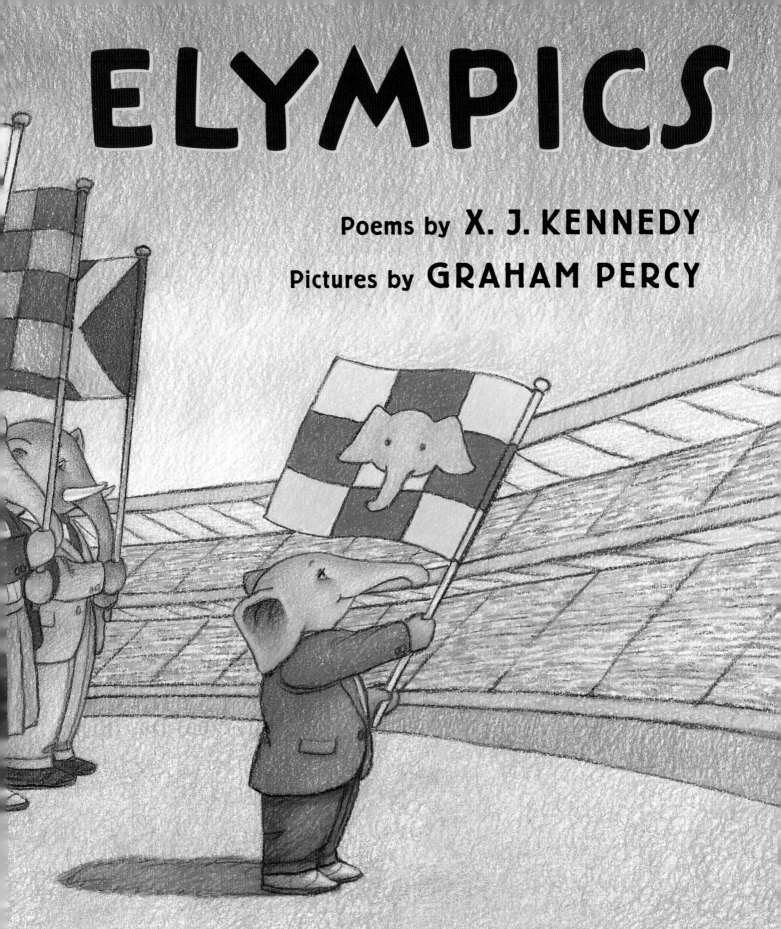

**Philomel Books • New York**

# SUMMER

# GAMES

# Sprinting

Here's little Trinket finishing
The hundred-meter race
With seven others at her heels,
The wind warm in her face.

To gain a final burst of speed,
She flattens back her ears
And, inches from the finish line,
Amid loud rousing cheers,

She sticks her trunk way out in front
Like a long gray garden hose,
For Trinket is the very best
At winning by a nose.

# Triathalon

He swims, he runs, he rides a bike!
He speeds to beat the band!
He almost moves as fast, it seems,
On water as on land.

At last! Here's Tristram coming in
As hard as he can pedal
To flash across the finish line.
Hooray! A silver medal!

In fact, because he swam and ran
And biked, it seems to me
That Tristram shouldn't win ONE prize—
Has he not earned all three?

# Volleyball

To boost the ball across the net,
Eliza helps Lenore,
For teamwork (as all teammates know)
Is what it takes to score.

Now, if you hadn't seen them play,
You'd think, "What clumsy lunks!"
But watched in action, they display
Fast feet and well-trained trunks.

You want to hear some volleyballs
Go BANG like cannon crackers?
Just ask Eliza or Lenore—
They're wonderful ball-whackers!

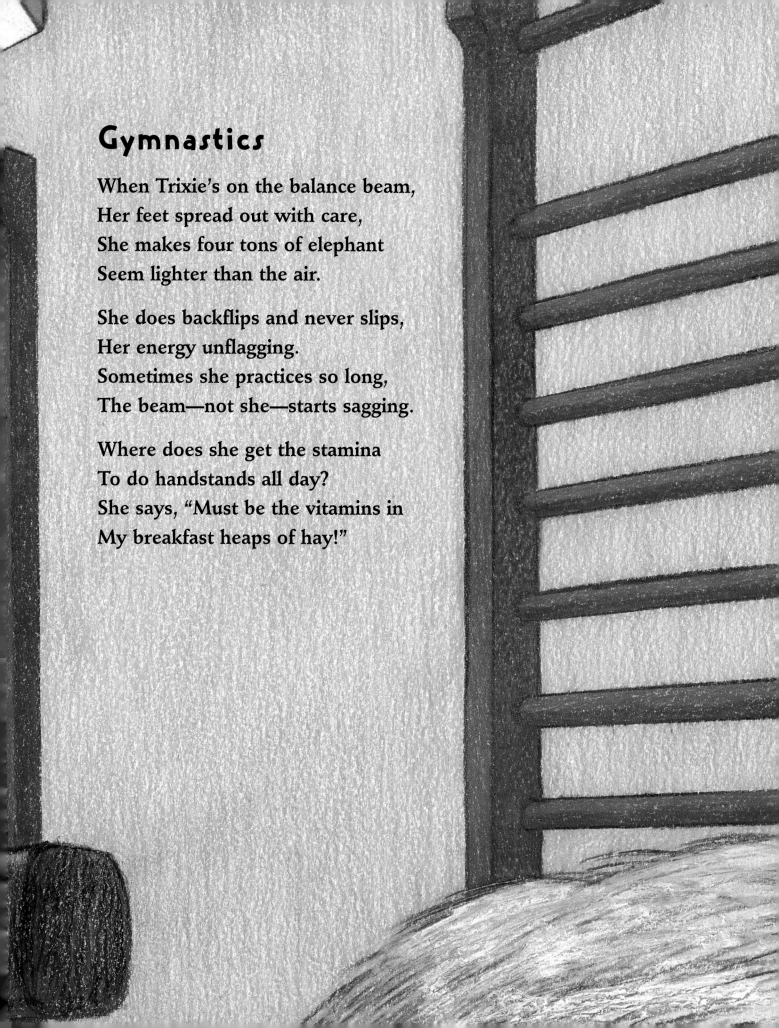

# Gymnastics

When Trixie's on the balance beam,
Her feet spread out with care,
She makes four tons of elephant
Seem lighter than the air.

She does backflips and never slips,
Her energy unflagging.
Sometimes she practices so long,
The beam—not she—starts sagging.

Where does she get the stamina
To do handstands all day?
She says, "Must be the vitamins in
My breakfast heaps of hay!"

# Diving

While bounding from his diving board
And somersaulting down,
Elijah keeps on worrying—
His forehead wears a frown.

He worries, "Was that takeoff good?
Supposing I arrive
A second later than I should
And do a messy dive?"

Elijah worries needlessly.
Thanks to hard work and training,
The judges score his dive a TEN.
That's perfect. Who's complaining?

# Hammer

To hurl his heavy hammer far,
Here's muscular Trelawney.
For this event you have to be
Huge, powerful, and brawny.

And yet who'd think an elephant
The same size as your house
Could be half scared out of his skin
By Mozzarella Mouse?

"EEK! EEK! I see a mouse!" he shrieks—
He makes the whole crowd smile,
And yet, though scared, Trelawney throws
His hammer one whole mile!

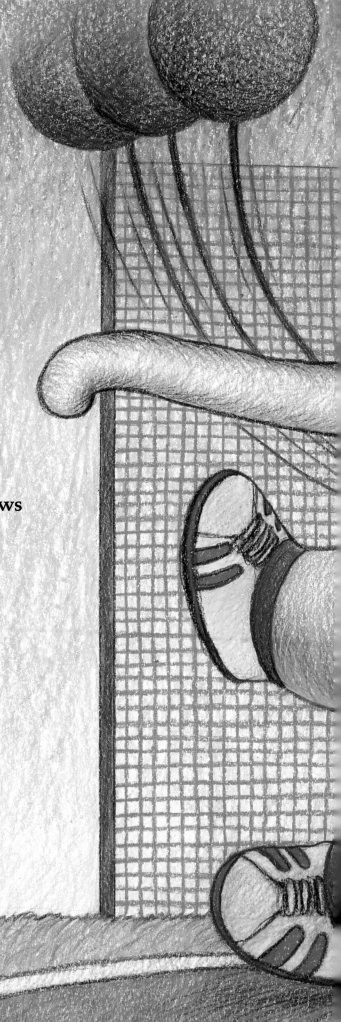

## High Jump

"Why, who would dream I'd make the team!"
Cried Ella in dismay.
"A great big lump like me can't jump—
My knees won't work that way."

"Now, Ella, please—forget your knees.
Just jump!" her coach replied.
"You won't believe what you'll achieve
Till you've gone out and tried."

So Ella worked, and every day,
With hopeful heart hard pumping,
Up from the floor she rose still more
And soon began high-jumping.

Now she's a star. Across the bar
She soars with birdlike grace—
Well, wouldn't you be grinning, too,
If you were in her place?

# WINTER

# GAMES

# Figure Skating

When Elfantina whirls and glides,
She's practicing to slice
(As figure skaters like to do)
A number in the ice.

She spins 'round, doing triple twirls,
And sprays you with ice crystals—
You'd think that you'd been squirted by
Six frozen water pistols!

Oh, isn't it a wonder that
Her whole half-ton of weight
Can balance, light as starlight, on
The tiptoe of a skate?

# Ski Jump

Big Elmo gobbled down a ton
Of peanuts and grew snoozy,
So when he came to make his jump
He felt a wee bit woozy.

He took off smoothly through the air,
But—oh-oh—when he landed
He hit a snowbank upside down.
He'll end up empty handed.

Poor Elmo. There go all his hopes
To be a medal winner.
If YOU ski-jump on snowy slopes,
Don't eat a ton for dinner.

# Bobsled

Swift as the wind, Eileen and Trish,
Two tusky girls in goggles,
Take a bobsled ride down a slippery slide
All bumps and wiggle-woggles.

They lean to the left, they lean to the right—
While jetting down, they're getting
Their balance right—girls, don't wipe out!
That might be too upsetting.

They round a bend. They near the end.
Officials wave a checkered
Flag to tell all the world they've won!
They've set a new speed record!

Why are they champs? They've practiced hard
In frosty winter weather,
And now they're like twin sister birds
Who've learned to sing together.

# Ice Hockey

On flashing skates Tremendous skims.
Who'd think a roly-poly
Big as a truck could lash a puck
And smash it past the goalie?

Poor goalie. Surely he must cringe
To see that giant frame
Come roaring down the hockey rink
And straight at him take aim.

Who'd think, to see Tremendous play,
That he was kind of shy?
But just remove him from the ice
And—what a gentle guy!

## Slalom

While whizzing down a mountainside
At top speed, Tram looks solemn
Because he hopes to do his best
In his event, the slalom.

Wild wolfish winds howl at his back—
See how he zigs and zags
And skillfully zooms in and out
Between the fluttering flags.

But Tram's not one to boast. He'll say,
When called the Slalom King,
"Shucks, all I did was go downhill
Not hitting anything."

# Medal Winner

O day of triumph! Here's Trumpette
Collecting her reward,
The brightest medal athletes get,
A gold one on a cord.

Now all her cares seem far away,
Those long hard months of trying—
Whoever thought she'd see this day?
She's on the brink of crying

With joy. Her name will live in fame,
For elephants don't forget.
Gold medals glitter, but a name
That lives is brighter yet.

*For Emily,*
*with mammoth affection—*X.J.K.

*For Taio—*G.P.

*Patricia Lee Gauch, editor*

Text copyright © 1999 by X. J. Kennedy
Illustrations copyright © 1999 by Graham Percy
Philomel Books, a division of Penguin Putnam Books for Young Readers,
345 Hudson Street, New York, NY, 10014. Philomel Books, Reg. U.S. Pat. & Tm. Off.
Published simultaneously in Canada. Printed in Hong Kong by South China Printing Co. (1988) Ltd.
Book design by Marikka Tamura. The text is set in Stempel Schneidler Bold.
The art was done using watercolor and colored pencils on Roberson cartridge paper.

Library of Congress Cataloging-in-Publication Data
Kennedy, X. J. Elympics / X. J. Kennedy ; illustrated by Graham Percy   p.  cm.
Summary: Elephants compete in a variety of sports, such as diving, triathlon, hammer throw, and figure skating.
[1. Sports—Fiction.  2. Elephants—Fiction.  3. Stories in rhyme.]  I. Percy, Graham, ill.  II. Title.
PZ8.3.K384E1 1999 [E]—dc21    98-20579    CIP AC   ISBN 0-399-23249-4
1  3  5  7  9  10  8  6  4  2
First Impression

## Author's Note

The Olympic games represent all that is good about sports and competition. For two celebratory weeks every two years, alternating between summer and winter games, athletes from nations around the world look past the color of each other's skin, forget about wars present and past, and unite in a spirit of friendship. The athletes want to win a gold medal more than anything, but should they lose, the experience of competing against the best in the world makes a winner out of everyone.

The very first Olympic games are thought to have been held around 1400 B.C. The event was a simple festival held among the Greeks to honor their gods, and held none of the grand spectacle of the modern games. The first recorded Olympic contest took place in Olympia, Greece, in 776 B.C. Years later an earthquake destroyed the Stadium of Olympia, and the games were stopped. It wasn't until the year 1896 that the modern Olympic games were reestablished, making them only a little more than a hundred years old.

The modern games are symbolized by five interlocking rings representing the continents of Africa, Asia, Australia, Europe, and the Americas (North and South). The rings are black, blue, green, red, and yellow. The flag of every nation competing in the games has at least one of these colors.

Athletes train for years and years in order to compete in the Olympics. It takes an intense dedication and love of practice in order to be good enough. Those that persevere are rewarded with the experience of a lifetime—representing their country, and themselves, in the Olympic games.

—*X. J. K.*